Zombies Ate My Homework

Paul Wennersberg-Løvholen

ISBN: 978-82-93748-44-1 (hardback)
ISBN: 978-82-93748-46-5 (paperback)
ISBN: 978-82-93748-47-2 (kindle)
ISBN: 978-82-93748-45-8 (ebook)

DEDICATION

Thanks to everyone who helped bring this book to life, especially my own little monsters, Amelia and Luna, who are my both my biggest critics and biggest inspiration.

CONTENTS

1	The Outlandish Excuse	1
2	The New Teacher	6
3	Something Fishy	11
4	Classroom Craziness	15
5	Lunchtime Lunacy	18
6	Worm Watch	21
7	What Does the Box Say	24
8	A Little Too Nosy	28
9	Seeking the Werewolf	36
10	Tale of the Werewolf Teacher	42
11	Planning in the Moonlight	46
12	Wiggly Wriggles and Wavy Waves	50
13	The Sound of Freedom	54

CONTENTS

14	Night Whispers	59
15	Club Origins	63
16	Dawn at Danger's Door	71
17	Art Attack	75
18	The Worm Turns	79
19	Wormageddon	85
20	Men in Black	88
21	Back to the Grind	93
22	Myths and Monsters	97
23	The Ultimate Excuse	100
24	The Mysterious Note	104

CHAPTER 1

THE OUTLANDISH EXCUSE

The morning sun streamed through the large classroom windows, illuminating the space with a soft, golden light. It highlighted the desks filled with colorful pencil cases, open books, and neatly stacked homework sheets—except for one desk. Lila, a petite girl whose vibrant personality was as untamable as her crown of messy curls, shifted in her seat under the watchful gaze of Mrs. Cobb. The teacher, known for her stern demeanor and a seemingly permanent half-frown, paced methodically between the rows of desks.

Stopping beside Lila, Mrs. Cobb inquired in her strict tone, "And where, pray tell, is your homework, Lila?"

Feeling the weight of her classmates' curious eyes, Lila swallowed hard. Yet, a spark of mischief danced in her bright, expressive eyes as she began her tale. "Well, Mrs. Cobb, it's quite the story," she said, twirling a curl around her finger, embodying the spirit of a born storyteller. "You see, just as I finished my homework last night, ready to tuck it safely in my bag, a UFO descended right into my backyard. Aliens, curious about Earth's educational system, borrowed my homework to study our mathematics!"

A ripple of laughter spread through the classroom. Mrs. Cobb raised an eyebrow, clearly unimpressed. "Aliens, Lila? Is that the best we can do today?"

Beside her, Max, Lila's best friend and partner in all things adventurous, couldn't help but join in. His wheelchair, which he maneuvered with practiced ease, bore stickers of spaceships, zombies, and other tokens of their shared escapades. "Maybe they needed help with their spaceship's fuel calculations?" he suggested, playing along with a grin.

Lila pointed at Max, nodding enthusiastically. "Exactly! They assured me they'd return it by today. Said it was crucial for intergalactic diplomacy, or something along those lines."

Mrs. Cobb's expression softened momentarily, a glimpse of amusement breaking through. "While I appreciate your creativity, Lila, I would much rather you applied that mind of yours to actually completing your assignments. Remember, imagination is a gift, but responsibility is key."

A bit sheepish but not entirely disheartened, Lila offered a quiet apology. "I'm sorry, Mrs. Cobb. I'll have it by tomorrow, promise."

Mrs. Cobb nodded, her attention turning to the day's lesson plan. However, before she could delve into the intricacies of arithmetic or the mysteries of history, she had an announcement that piqued the entire class's interest.

"We'll be welcoming a new teacher to our school today. He's set to take over Mr. Smyth's classroom next door."

Lila's curiosity was instantly ignited, her mind whirling with possibilities. Leaning towards Max, she whispered conspiratorially, "A new teacher? Do you think he might be in league with those homework-borrowing extraterrestrials?"

Max's laughter was soft but filled with excitement. "Or perhaps he's an intergalactic ambassador disguised as a teacher, ensuring all homework reaches the correct galaxy. We've got a mystery to unravel!"

Their laughter was like a secret handshake, something special just between them. It showed just how tight they were, like two peas in a pod or, better yet, two explorers ready for their next big quest. Lila and Max had been through a lot together. From the "Haunted Playground Mystery" to the "Case of the Missing Cookies", they'd seen it all. Or so they thought.

Max was always ready with a clever plan or a funny joke to lighten the mood. Being in a wheelchair never slowed him down; in fact, Lila thought it made him even braver. He had this amazing way of looking at the world, like every day was a new adventure waiting to happen.

Lila, always a whirlwind of energy and ideas, found in Max the perfect partner-in-crime. Her wild curls were a perfect match for her wild ideas, and where she jumped in headfirst, Max was right there beside her, figuring out how to land safely.

As Mrs. Cobb went back to talking about homework and history, Max and Lila were already whispering about aliens and secret agents. The idea of a new teacher stirred up all kinds of exciting possibilities. "What if he's a spy?" Lila mused, eyes sparkling with the thrill of a new mystery.

Max grinned, adding, "Or maybe he really is an alien in disguise, sent to learn about Earth kids!"

They both giggled, not because they really believed in alien teachers or spy missions, but because imagining wild stories was their favorite thing to do. It made every day an adventure, even if it was just a regular day at school.

Little did they know their jokes about the new teacher would soon lead them into one of their biggest adventures yet. As they packed up their bags, still chuckling about space missions and homework-stealing aliens, they didn't notice the new teacher stood outside their classroom looking in and watching them with a mysterious smile.

CHAPTER 2

THE NEW TEACHER

As the bell's ring dissipated, a buzz of youthful energy spilled into the halls. Stories of weekend escapades faded as Lila tugged at Max's sleeve, her eyes alight with a mix of mischief and curiosity. "Max, quick! Let's check out the new teacher before the next class," she whispered, her voice tinged with excitement.

Max grinned, maneuvering his wheelchair effortlessly beside her. "Lead the way, Detective Lila!"

The two friends went outside and positioned themselves where they could easily see in to the to the classroom window, hopefully without being seen themselves A tall man stood by the teacher's desk, meticulously arranging what appeared to be vials filled with strange-coloured liquids. Unlike anything they'd expected, Mr. Xanar was a sight to behold.

He was dressed in a suit that seemed too elegant for a school setting, with a dark, velvety blazer that contrasted sharply with the bright, classroom lights. His pants were a shade of deep purple, unusual yet oddly captivating. The most striking feature, however, were his socks-not glowing, but patterned with vibrant, swirling colors that seemed to dance as he moved. Around his neck, a tie shifted through a kaleidoscope of colors, changing with every turn he took.

Lila nudged Max, barely containing her excitement. "Look at his socks! And that tie... it's like a rainbow in motion!"

Max peered closer. "He's definitely not from around here. Who dresses like that for school?"

As they observed, Mr. Xanar turned, catching a glimpse of his profile. He wore round spectacles that magnified his eyes, giving him an inquisitive look. "I am Mr. Xanar," he announced to the empty room, practicing his introduction. His voice, deep and resonant, filled the space with an unusual timbre.

Lila and Max exchanged amused looks. "Mr. Xanar, the Extra-terrestrial Expert of Fashion?" Lila quipped, trying to stifle her laughter.

Suddenly, as if feeling the weight of their gaze, Mr. Xanar turned sharply towards the window. His eyes, magnified by the round glasses, met theirs. The brief eye contact sent a shiver down their spines, a mix of thrill and fear.

The door to Mr. Xanar's classroom burst open, admitting a stream of pupils, breaking the tense moment. Mr. Xanar greeted the pupils coming in with a nod, turning away from the window, his attention now fully on his new class.

Lila and Max, hearts still racing from the unexpected encounter, knew it was time to head back. As they retreated, the bell rang through the corridors, signaling the start of a new lesson and marking the end of their brief reconnaissance mission.

"Well," Max breathed out, a grin spreading across his face despite the adrenaline, "Mr. Xanar is either the most eccentric teacher Swindon has ever seen or there's more to him than meets the eye."

Lila nodded, the wheels in her mind already turning. "Either way, we've got our next mystery."

Their brief encounter with Mr. Xanar had opened the door to a new adventure, one that promised to be as intriguing as it was unexpected. As they made their way back to class, the image of Mr. Xanar's intense, magnified gaze stayed with them, hinting at the mysteries to come.

CHAPTER 3

SOMETHING FISHY

Lila and Max made their way to their next lesson- science with Mr. Lunis. They were the last pupils to arrive, and Lila mumbled an apology to Mr. Lunis before they found their places in the classroom. Today's topic was on aquatic ecosystems, and the class was abuzz with excitement as they got to observe their classroom aquarium, brimming with exotic fish and vibrant plants.

Max had a passion for fish and all things aquatic. Leaning close to the glass, he studied each fish with great interest. "Hey, Lila, around 95% of the sea is unexplored. If you're looking for aliens and mysterious creatures, you really don't need to travel to another planet." He jotted down notes, sketched some of the more intricate patterns, and occasionally looked up to share a fun fact with Lila.

"Did you know, Lila, that some fish communicate with electrical signals?" he remarked, pointing to a tiny, almost translucent fish darting around a rock.

Lila smirked. "Well, I communicate with exaggerated facial expressions," she said pulling a ridiculous face. "Equally impressive, don't you think?"

Max chuckled but was quickly drawn back to the tank, his eyes narrowing as they caught sight of something unusual. A small, worm-like creature, almost resembling a translucent noodle, was slowly slinking its way up the aquarium's glass wall. Its movements were unlike any aquatic creature he had seen before; it moved in sharp, abrupt jolts, sometimes twirling as if caught in a personal whirlwind.

"Uh, Lila?" Max said, pointing to the creature. "Have you ever seen something like this?"

Lila leaned in, her eyebrows knitting together. "No... It doesn't look like any fish I've seen. It's more like... a worm?"

Just then, they both observed the worm-like entity shoot up to the water's surface, expanding and contracting rapidly. A tiny bubble formed around its head and then, to their astonishment, the creature launched itself out of the water, landing on a leaf of a nearby plant. The way it maneuvered wasn't natural, it was... otherworldly.

Lila gulped; her playful demeanor replaced by genuine concern. "That's not normal, Max."

Max nodded, his eyes never leaving the creature. "It's almost as if it's trying to adapt, learn... evolve."

"Evolve? Like an alien?" Lila whispered, her thoughts immediately racing back to Mr. Xanar and his peculiar attire. Could there be a connection?

Max rolled his eyes. "Not everything strange is an alien, Lila. Like I said, a lot of these sea creatures could be considered alien to us. The sea is full of oddities."

Lila shot him a mischievous grin. "Oh, come on! After seeing Mr. Xanar's glowing clothes and this worm doing the cha-cha, I'd say anything's possible!"

Max chuckled, but the amusement quickly faded as he watched the worm closely. "We need to find out more about this creature. For all we know, it could be dangerous."

Lila nodded, determination lighting up her eyes. "Then it's a good thing Swindon Academy has its very own paranormal investigators. The adventure begins, Max!"

The two shared a fist bump, and in that moment, as they looked away, the mysterious creature vanished.

"Hey where did it go?" asked Max.

"I don't know," replied Lila, "but I don't like it."

Little did they know that this small worm was just the tip of a very large, extraterrestrial iceberg.

CHAPTER 4

CLASSROOM CRAZINESS

Lila and Max sat side by side, their attention still very much focused on the aquarium and the peculiar worm-like creature. However, they were soon distracted from their search for the missing worm, as this wasn't the only strange occurrence in science class that day.

Phillip, a typically docile boy with a passion for collecting rocks, was at his desk... eating paper. He wasn't just nibbling at it either; he was devouring sheet after sheet with a voracity that would make a goat envious.

Lila nudged Max and pointed discreetly towards Phillip. "I know we were asked to digest our lessons, but I think Phillip's taking it a bit too literally."

Max's eyes widened. "That's... certainly different."

Before they could dwell on Phillip's peculiar new appetite, another oddity caught their attention. Emily, the class poet, and a stickler for grammar, was standing on her chair and reciting the day's date... backwards.

"Two-thousand and twenty-three, ten, seventeen! Two-thousand and twenty-three, ten, seventeen!" she chanted repeatedly, her voice taking on an eerie monotone.

Max leaned towards Lila, whispering, "Okay, even for Emily, that's strange. Maybe she's practicing for a 'Backwards Day' poem?"

Lila frowned, concern evident in her eyes. "Max, first Mr. Xanar, then the worm, and now this? I know I have an overactive imagination at times, but something is definitely up."

Just then, the door flew open, revealing Mr. Lunis. His shaggy, unkempt hair was even more unkempt, if that were possible, his tie was askew, and instead of his usual clipboard and pen, he was carrying a potted plant. And, instead of the usual greeting, he seemed more preoccupied with the plant than his students.

"Good, uh, morning," he started, seemingly

distracted, "I believe this plant needs... sunlight," he mumbled, more to himself than to the class.

Lila and Max exchanged a look of disbelief, their thoughts mirroring each other's - the school was definitely caught in a wave of weirdness.

Without warning, the lights in the classroom flickered, not once, but thrice, casting shadows that danced across the walls. A collective gasp filled the room as the students looked around, bewildered.

Mr. Lunis, plant still in hand, surveyed the room, a sigh escaping him. "It seems," he paused, "that perhaps we're all in need of a break. Let's, um, reconvene after an early lunch."

Max looked around at the chaos enveloping their usually predictable classroom. "We need to get to the bottom of this."

Lila nodded; her adventurous spirit reignited. "I told you something was up. Let's start our investigation at lunch. We have a mystery to solve!"

The duo exchanged a determined nod, gearing up for the oddest day of their lives.

CHAPTER 5

LUNCHTIME LUNACY

Lunchtime had always been Lila and Max's favorite part of the day, a time when the 'Zombies Ate My Homework Club' convened in the canteen to discuss their latest silly conspiracies, spooky suspicions, or whatever strange news they had read. Today, however, the canteen was a tad more bizarre than they were used to.

Lila held up her tray, scrutinizing the lime green, wobbly jelly that had been served. It wasn't just jiggling - it was pulsating like a mini trampoline. She poked it with a fork, and to her astonishment, the jelly squeaked in protest.

Max looked over, raising an eyebrow. "You

know, if that jelly starts tap dancing, I'm out of here."

Lila chuckled. "You know what they say, Max. There's always room for dancing jelly, although in this case I may just give it a miss," pushing the jelly aside.

Lila's playful demeanor faded as she took in the peculiarities of the lunchroom. Pupils were chatting, but their voices were off-pitch, almost robotic. One girl had her shoes on her hands, clapping them together in applause whenever anyone spoke. Another boy had fashioned a makeshift crown from bananas and proclaimed himself the "King of Fruits."

Even Lila, with her love for the bizarre, found it hard to find the humor in the situation. She leaned in close to Max, her voice low. "I've always said that school can be a bit 'strange' at times, but this is... too much."

Max nodded; his gaze serious. "I agree. We need to figure out what's going on, Lila. It's not just funny anymore; it's concerning."

The duo made their way through the chaotic lunchroom, trying to piece together the puzzle. As they passed a group of their friends, they couldn't help but overhear snippets of conversations that were... well, not conversations at all.

"Ice cream, stapler, umbrella!" declared one pupil emphatically.

"Moon cheese, bicycle frog, hiccup!" responded another, nodding sagely.

Lila sighed, "This is just bonkers."

Max frowned, thinking. "It's like their brains are scrambled or were being controlled by something."

Lila's eyes widened as a thought struck her. "The worm! What if it's... I don't know, releasing something into the water? Affecting everyone? Maybe there are more of them!"

Max considered the idea. "It's possible. But we need evidence. We need to find that worm!"

Lila nodded, determination burning in her eyes. "Let's pay a visit to that aquarium after lunch. Something tells me our little wormy friend might be the key to all this craziness."

As the pair made their plans, the lunchroom around them grew even wilder, but beneath the silliness, an eerie undercurrent ran deep. Something was amiss, but Lila and Max were on the case.

CHAPTER 6

WORM WATCH

The school bell rang, signaling that lunch had finished and afternoon lessons were about to begin. However, for Lila and Max, their real class had just begun: Detective 101.

As pupils rushed past, the duo stood against a wall, observing their classmates' peculiar behaviors. They took note of which pupils seemed the most affected by the oddities. None of the pupils affected seemed to have anything in common, besides behaving like they'd been zapped by the wacky-ray. Lila and Max quickly returned to Mr. Lunis' class in search of the aquarium and the mysterious worm. But when they arrived there was no sign of the class aquarium. Just a blank space on the shelf where it once stood.

"Ummm, Mr. Lunis," said Lila, getting her teachers attention. "What happened to the fish tank?"

Mr. Lunis, who seemed lost in a world of his own, slowly raised his head. "The fish tank has been moved to Mr. Xanar's class for the remainder of this term for a special project, apparently."

Lila's eyes twinkled with a mix of mischief and determination as she turned to Max. "I told you Mr. Xanar was fishy! First, the new teacher, then the worm, then all this craziness."

Max sighed. "It's a connection, but it's not concrete proof. We need to find out what is happening in that classroom. We need a plan."

"Ummm but shouldn't you two be elsewhere?" enquired Mr. Lunis.

Mr. Lunis was right. History with Mrs. Cobb. The duo left a seemingly distracted Mr. Lunis alone in his classroom and then made their way to History class.

Now Mrs. Cobb had a certain knack for making even the most interesting subjects sound insanely boring. So, whilst all the other pupils listened to her droning on about the great pyramids, and people having their brains pulled out of their noses with hooks, the duo whispered and plotted quietly in the corner.

After a lot of back and forth discussing the day's events and trying to settle on their next course of action, Lila's face lit up. "What if one of us hides in Mr. Xanar's class before class tomorrow and spies to see what's going on?"

Max gulped. "It sounds a bit risky. Plus, I don't think I'm going to be able to hide this," he said gesturing towards his wheelchair. "How about we spy on him from our hideout. We can see perfectly into Mrs. Cobbs class from there and Mr. Xanar is just next door!"

Lila grinned, ready for the adventure. "You're right, Detective Max, Operation Worm-Watch is a go! Let's uncover the mystery of Mr. Xanar and save our classmates!"

As the two plotted and planned, they felt the weight of their responsibility. They weren't just dealing with forgotten homework or cheeky classroom antics anymore. They were battling a mystery that threatened to turn their school upside down. Were they ready for the challenge?

CHAPTER 7

WHAT DOES THE BOX SAY

The next morning Lila and Max had both arrived extra early to school, long before the bell was due to ring in signaling first class, and they made their way to their secret clubhouse. The hideout of the Zombies Ate My Homework Club was in a dusty old storage shed next to the school gym. It was filled with old sports equipment, crates, and, to any outsider, it looked like a mess. But to Lila and Max, it was a haven for plotting, scheming, and connecting the dots of their paranormal investigations. And the best thing about it was that it had seemingly been forgotten. Not a soul besides Lila and Max ever went there, besides the occasional visit from Juno, the caretakers scruffy one-eyed cat.

Next to one of the shed windows, Max had installed an old telescope they had found in a charity shop, perfect for spying. And luckily for them this window had a clear view into both Mrs. Cobbs and Mr. Xanar's classroom, making it an excellent vantage point. As they watched and waited for Mr. Xanar to show up in his classroom, Lila began reminiscing.

"Do you remember, Max," she giggled, "when we thought Mrs. Paddleton was a vampire because she always wore those big, dark sunglasses indoors?"

Max chuckled. "Oh, yes! And then it turned out she just had an eye infection."

Lila continued, "Or that time we were convinced Mr. Thompson was becoming a mummy because of the bandage on his hand?"

Max grinned. "He'd just cut himself chopping vegetables! But I'll admit that one had me going for a bit."

The two shared a laugh, but the atmosphere turned serious as they looked through the periscope and saw Mr. Xanar walk into the room. Lila's eyes narrowed.

"This time it's different, Max," she

whispered. "This isn't about someone wearing sunglasses or having a bandage. Pupils are acting strange, well stranger than normal. And I don't think this is just a case of a teacher with an eccentric dress sense."

Max nodded. "I agree. Whatever's going on with Mr. Xanar, we need to get to the bottom of it."

As they watched, a pupil named Samira entered the classroom. Mr. Xanar closed the door behind her, his movements deliberate and slightly unnatural. The room seemed to darken just a touch, and a slight chill ran down Lila's spine.

Max adjusted the telescope to get a better view. "Look! He's taking out something from his desk drawer."

Lila squinted, trying to get a better look. "It's... it's a small box. And there's something glowing inside!"

Both kids were entranced by the soft, eerie light emanating from the box. As Mr. Xanar opened it, the glow intensified, bathing Samira in its luminescence. Her eyes went blank, her posture rigid.

Max's voice trembled. "This isn't like our past theories, Lila. This is real."

Lila clenched her fists, determination setting in. "We need to find out what's in that box and how to stop Mr. Xanar."

As they continued to watch, both friends knew that they were no longer playing at being detectives. They were dealing with something far beyond their wildest imaginings, and the stakes had never been higher.

CHAPTER 8

A LITTLE TOO NOSY

From their secret lookout, Lila and Max were engrossed in the scene unfolding before them. Samira, previously glowing under the light of the mysterious box, stood motionless. Mr. Xanar approached her, holding a tiny glass container. Inside the container, a slender worm-like creature wriggled, its tiny form contrasting starkly with the terror it represented.

"Max," Lila whispered, gripping the edge of their makeshift desk, "that looks just like the worm from the aquarium!"

Before Max could respond, they watched in horror as Mr. Xanar carefully opened the container. The worm slithered out, moving with a determined, sinister Samira. To the duo's growing terror, it made its way to Samira's nose and, with a quick, snaking motion, disappeared up one her nostrils.

"No..." Max breathed, his face pale.

Samira's transformation was instantaneous. Her posture shifted from rigid to relaxed, her eyes once vacant now glowed with a strange luminescence similar to the box's eerie light. A slight smile played on her lips, but it wasn't the innocent smile of a schoolgirl. It was something more sinister, more knowing.

Lila gulped. "That wasn't just a worm, Max. That was some kind of alien parasite."

Max nodded slowly; his eyes fixed on Samira as she conversed animatedly with Mr. Xanar. "And now she's one of them. Whatever 'them' is."

The implications of what they'd witnessed were vast. Their fellow pupils weren't just acting weird – they were being invaded, controlled. But by whom? And why?

Lila's ever-active mind raced. "We have to find a way to save them. Think, Max! We've seen movies and read books. There must be a way to get those creatures out without hurting anyone!"

Max pondered for a moment, recalling an article he had read in The Weekly Weird News. "So, you know how dogs react to high frequencies?"

"You mean those whistles that drive them crazy?"

"Exactly!" said Max. "All creatures react to different sound frequencies in different ways. The CIA actually conducted secret experiments with sound waves to control people. They even invented one called The Brown Sound."

"What did that do?" asked Lila.

"You really do not want to know" answered Max, "there was a reason they called it The Brown Sound, but my point is that maybe, just maybe, the right frequency could force the worms out."

Lila clapped her hands, her energy infectious. "You are brilliant, Max! But we need more information. We need to find out where these worms come from and why they're here."

The duo settled into their chairs; their mission clear. With every passing second, their resolve strengthened. They had witnessed the unimaginable, and now they had to act.

Lila peeked through the telescope one last time, watching as Samira exited the room, her steps more deliberate, her demeanor completely altered. "We're going to save them, Max. All of them."

And with that declaration, the two friends began to lay out their plan, a mix of audacity, bravery, and the hope that they could make a difference.

Lila and Max, still in their hideout, couldn't shake the chill that ran down their spines after witnessing Samira's transformation. There was an unsettling silence between the two, as if speaking about it would somehow make the situation even more real.

Max was the first to break the silence. "Lila... did that really just happen?"

Lila nodded solemnly; her usual vivacity dimmed by the gravity of the situation. "Sure, looked like it. Poor Samira. One moment she's thinking about her next maths assignment and the next, she's... alien-zombified."

Max shivered. "It's like one of those horror movies, only scarier because it's real."

A few moments passed, the gravity of their reality weighing them down before Lila's face lit up. “You know,” she began, tapping her chin thoughtfully, “you’d think if aliens were advanced enough to travel light-years across space, they’d come up with a better entrance than the nose. I mean, how unglamorous!”

“Well, it could be much worse!” said Max, looking down. He chuckled despite himself. “They must have been paying attention to Mrs. Cobbs class yesterday.”

“Well at least someone was!” joked Lila, “I mean, if I were an alien, I’d at least choose something cool like... I don’t know, a magical twirl or a spectacular light show. Not the nostril slide.”

Max laughed harder, feeling the tension in the room lift a little. “The nostril slide! That’s a good one, Lila.”

She grinned, her spark returning. “Always here to put a comedic spin on our impending doom. It’s a gift, really.”

It was moments like these that Max cherished. Even in the darkest situations, Lila had a knack for finding a sliver of humor. It wasn’t just about making light of the situation; it was about reminding themselves that even when faced with unimaginable horrors, they had each other. And together, they could find a way to push through.

"Well," Max said, his tone more serious, "whatever entrance they choose, we need to find an exit for those worms. And soon."

Lila nodded, determination flashing in her eyes. "Agreed. We need a plan, and fast. Time to put our heads together and come up with something brilliant."

Max wheeled himself to the corner of their hideout, searching through the pile of miscellaneous items they'd collected over the years for their various investigations. Lila, her brain working a mile a minute, was pacing back and forth.

"We need to find a way to fight these worm things," she said, more to herself than to Max. "Some kind of weakness. But what?"

Max pulled out a notebook from under a pile. "Remember this?" he asked, holding up a dusty book with 'Teacher Theories' scribbled on the cover.

Lila grinned. "Oh, our old research! I'd forgotten about this." She plopped down next to Max, flipping open the notebook to a random page. "Ha! Mrs. Beaker, a suspected zombie for her extreme paleness and penchant for red juice. Turns out she just had an iron deficiency and a love for cranberry juice."

They both giggled, the levity of their past theories providing a temporary escape. But as they continued flipping, they reached a section that stopped them cold.

"Mr. Lunis, the Science Teacher," Lila read aloud. "Suspected werewolf."

Max's eyes widened. "I remember that. He always had those furry hands and wouldn't come to school on full moon nights."

Lila nodded. "Exactly. And didn't he always have this odd howling ringtone?"

The memories flooded back, reminding them of the many lunchtimes they'd spent secretly observing Mr. Lunis in his science lab, trying to catch him in his werewolf form.

Max chewed his lip thoughtfully. "Lila, do you think it's possible? If Mr. Lunis really is a werewolf, maybe he can help us. Werewolves have heightened senses, right? Maybe he's noticed something about Mr. Xanar that we haven't."

Lila's eyes sparkled with hope. "It's worth a shot. I mean, at this point, teaming up with a possible werewolf is our best bet."

Max gave her a mock salute. "To seeking the

werewolf, then."

Lila smirked, adding, "And hoping he's on our side and not too furry."

CHAPTER 9

SEEKING THE WEREWOLF

That evening, the moon over Swindon was nearly full, painting a silver glow on the streets below. Perfect timing for a visit to a suspected werewolf's house, thought Lila. She'd managed to find Mr. Lunis's address in a school directory that she had 'borrowed' from the office.

Attached to Max's wheelchair, a series of small motion sensors and lights, meant to alert them if anything, or anyone, came too close. They were actually meant to ward off cats from gardens, but Max was a genius with technology and had modified them into this early warning system. There was just one problem - Max and

Lila's own movements continuously triggered the sensors, so as Max wheeled down the road, he looked like some mobile disco, in contrast to the eerily silent night.

"I guess this takes away any element of surprise," remarked Lila.

"Well, at least we won't get hassled by any cats," joked Max, "though not sure how good it is with wolves. Lila, do you think this is a good idea? I mean, what if he's mid-transformation or something?"

Lila shrugged, her face a mask of faux confidence. "We've dealt with 'vampires' and 'zombies'. How bad can a werewolf be? Plus," she added with a smirk, "we've got garlic... and I may have borrowed a silver spoon from the kitchen."

Max chuckled. "Right, because in a showdown with a werewolf, we'll challenge him to a spoon fight."

"Call that a spoon! This is a spoon!" quipped Lila, whipping out the silverware, and quoting from an old film she'd watched.

The two friends made their way up the path leading to Mr. Lunis's old stone house, its pointed roof casting eerie shadows. Ivy crept up the walls like clawed hands, and every so often, an owl hooted from a nearby tree. The setting was straight out of a classic horror story, and Lila half-expected Dracula to greet them at the door.

Instead, when they gently knocked, it was the familiar face of Mr. Lunis, though now it bore a wilder look. His hair…had it grown longer, and those furry hands? Furrier than ever.

Mr. Lunis blinked in surprise. "Lila? Max? What are you doing here at this hour?"

Lila cleared her throat. "Well, sir, it's a bit of a long story. Do you have a moment? Or are you... busy?"

She eyed his furrier-than-usual hands, hoping he'd get the hint, and that if he were about to turn into a slobbering canine, he'd be too busy to invite them in. Instead, he smiled, revealing some exceptionally large canine teeth. Or was that just Lila's wild imagination playing tricks?

"Come on in," he said, opening the door wider. "But I warn you, midnight is usually my wild time, so you best make it quick!"

Max whispered to Lila as they entered, "If he starts howling, I'm using you as a shield."

Lila poked him in the side, laughing silently.

"Deal."

Inside Mr. Lunis's home, the dim light revealed walls lined with old, leather-bound books and peculiar, twisted plants that seemed to almost... move. Lila and Max exchanged glances, wondering if they had made the right decision to come here.

They sat down, and Lila began, "Sir, we think something weird is going on at school. And we think it might be... aliens."

Mr. Lunis raised an eyebrow, looking a mix between amused and concerned. "Aliens, you say?"

Max nodded, taking the lead. "Yeah, and it started when Mr. Xanar arrived. Kids are acting strange, and there's this worm thingy…"

Before he could finish, there was a sudden crash at the back door. They turned to see one of their classmates, Luna, eyes glazed over, moving in a jerky, zombie-like manner. Her voice was a monotone as she said, "You shouldn't be here."

Lila whispered, "It's one of them!"

Mr. Lunis stood up, positioning himself between the children and Luna. "This isn't good," he murmured.

Max, in a panic, asked, "Mr. Lunis, can you

help? You're not... ordinary, are you?"

Lila gulped, "Yeah, the whole 'night owl' thing, and the, um, furry hands?" She wiggled her fingers, imitating hairy knuckles.

Mr. Lunis hesitated for a moment, then took a deep breath. "You're right. I'm not just a Science Teacher. And it seems tonight is the perfect night to reveal my true nature."

As the moonlight filtered through the window, it cast a glow on Mr. Lunis. Slowly, his form began to change. His face elongated, fur sprouted, and in a matter of moments, a full-fledged, yet oddly distinguished-looking, werewolf stood in his place.

Lila's eyes widened, her initial shock giving way to a grin. "Well, that's one way to get out of marking homework."

But Luna, or the entity controlling her, didn't

seem to find the situation funny. She lunged forward. The werewolf-Mr. Lunis let out a growl, moving swiftly to block her path, his sharp claws at the ready.

In the ensuing chaos, Max spotted an old, intricate musical box on a shelf. Without thinking, he wound it up and released its haunting melody into the room. The notes, pure and penetrating, filled the air. Luna clutched her ears in pain, the sound unbearable to whatever controlled her. From her nose, the worm-like creature began to emerge, seeking to escape the unbearable melody.

Lila, thinking quickly, grabbed an old vase and trapped the worm inside. The effect was immediate; Luna slumped, dazed but seemingly back to her normal self.

Catching their breath, Lila turned to werewolf-Mr. Lunis, trying to inject her usual humor into the situation. "Well, sir, that was a... transformative experience for all of us."

Mr. Lunis, shifting back to his human form, smiled ruefully. "Indeed. I think we have a lot to discuss."

CHAPTER 10

TALE OF THE WEREWOLF TEACHER

The three sat in the dim light of Mr. Lunis's living room, an atmosphere of apprehension hanging in the air. Lila and Max exchanged glances, waiting for their Science Teacher to spill the beans.

Mr. Lunis sighed deeply, rubbing the bridge of his nose, "Okay, let's get this out in the open. I'm sure you two have a ton of questions."

Max shifted in his seat, "You think?"

Lila smirked, "You could say that. First one being, when's the next full moon? Just so we can, you know, plan our schedules around it."

Mr. Lunis chuckled, "You've always been cheeky, Lila. Alright, let me tell you how this all began..."

He took a deep breath, pausing a moment to gather his thoughts. "This all happened many years ago," he began, his voice low and reflective. "I was much younger, a student with a thirst for adventure. One night, under the spell of a brilliant full moon, my life changed forever." He paused, a distant look in his eyes as if he were visualizing the night. "The air was crisp, and a chilling wind whispered secrets only the moon could understand. As I wandered, lost in thought, the sudden appearance of an American backpacker shattered the night's calm. He was a peculiar sight — clothes ragged; eyes wild with fear."

Lila and Max leaned closer, hanging on to every word.

"He seemed desperate, haunted by something unseen. I approached, intent on offering aid, but was met with a gaze that froze me in place. His eyes... there was a feral glow to them, a warning I failed to heed. Before I knew what was happening, he lunged at me, biting my arm. And then, just as quickly as he'd appeared, he ran off. When I looked down, I saw that he had left behind his clothes. I'm not sure what was stranger- the fact that he bit me, or that he ran off in his birthday suit."

Lila couldn't resist, "So... you met an American werewolf in... Swindon?"

Mr. Lunis couldn't help but laugh, "That's one way to put it. Well, I put the incident behind me and had almost forgotten about it. Until about a month later"

"The next full moon!" exclaimed Lila.

"Precisely," answered Mr. Lunis. "One minute I was having a cup of coffee, and the next I'm chasing cars and peeing against lampposts!"

Max's face wrinkled in concern, "But if you're a werewolf... doesn't that mean... you know... you eat people?"

Lila shot Max a 'really?' look, but she too was curious.

Mr. Lunis raised his eyebrows playfully, "Ah, the age-old stereotype. Thankfully, I'm a vegetarian. And, with all these fake meat options available now, I've managed to keep my... urges... in check."

Lila's eyes twinkled with mischief, "So you've never eaten anyone?"

He grinned wickedly, leaning in closer, "Well, there was this one pupil, but they tasted absolutely terrible."

Max gulped, eyes widening, before noticing the playful glint in Mr. Lunis's eyes.

Lila playfully slapped Mr. Lunis's shoulder, "You really had us there!"

Mr. Lunis chuckled, "Always good to keep you pupils on your toes."

The atmosphere in the room lightened as they all shared a laugh, but they knew they had a bigger issue to address: the alien invasion.

CHAPTER 11

PLANNING IN THE MOONLIGHT

Lila, Max, and Mr. Lunis sat cross-legged in a circle on the floor. Strangely, despite being home to a werewolf, and the earlier intrusion, Lila and Max felt safe in Mr. Lunis's home. Looking around the rooms were full of odd trinkets and instruments that any werewolf-scientist might need.

"So, aliens and werewolves in one school?" Lila began, "Must be some sort of extraterrestrial hotspot or something."

Mr. Lunis shrugged, "Maybe they heard about the excellent cafeteria food."

Max rolled his eyes, "Very funny. But seriously, what could they possibly want here? Why Swindon of all the places? And why our school?"

Mr. Lunis leaned back, thinking. "Well, every invasion has a motive. Maybe they need something here?"

Lila mused aloud, "Like a resource? What could they possibly want in Swindon…maybe they like trains, or roundabouts?"

Max gave Lila a pointed look. "Or maybe they want to take over human minds for some reason. Remember the worm thing?"

Mr. Lunis nodded. "It's possible. They might be using the pupils as hosts for... whatever those worm-like creatures are. We need to figure it out."

Lila's eyes sparkled with determination, "And stop them!"

"But how?" Mr. Lunis asked, worry evident in his eyes.

"Max had this idea that maybe we could drive out the worms with some kind of noise or soundwave. It seemed to work when I dropped that plant," said Lila. "By the way I'm sorry about that."

"No need to worry," said Mr. Lunis, "I think a broken vase is the least of our worries." He then scratched his furry chin thoughtfully and held up the worm that was now safely secured in a jar. "The science lab at school has all the equipment we might need to research these creatures further. Maybe there's a way to counteract their effects."

Lila grinned, "A little alien dissection in the science lab? I'm in!"

Max gulped, "As long as it doesn't involve any more transformations..."

Mr. Lunis chuckled, "Don't worry, I've got that part covered."

Lila pulled out her notebook, scribbling furiously. "Alright, here's the plan: we meet tomorrow, first thing in the morning, in the science lab. We'll need to be sneaky; we don't want any alien-controlled pupils or teachers spotting us."

Max raised an eyebrow, "Early morning? But tomorrow's Saturday. You sure?"

Lila smirked, "Come on, Max. Saving the world requires some sacrifices."

Mr. Lunis nodded in agreement. "Alright, tomorrow, in the lab. Let's do this."

As they stood up, Max glanced at Lila, "You think we can pull this off?"

Lila grinned cheekily, nudging him, "With a werewolf on our side? Absolutely!"

The three shared one last determined glance

before parting ways, ready to face the mysteries of the next day.

CHAPTER 12

WIGGLY WRIGGLES AND WAVY WAVES

The science lab was always a wonderland for Lila and Max, even more so now with the sun just starting to rise, painting the room in golden hues. Rows of long tables covered in beakers, test tubes, and all manner of scientific equipment stood silent, waiting for the day's experiments.

Max, rubbing his eyes sleepily, yawned, "Why did we have to meet this early again?"

Lila smirked, "Early bird gets the worm, remember?"

"Very funny," Max replied, eyeing the small container in the center of the table. It contained the worm-like creature, wiggling eerily.

Mr. Lunis, now back in his human form, adjusted his glasses. "Alright, let's get down to it. From our observations yesterday, we have determined that these creatures might be sensitive to certain frequencies of sound."

Lila looked curious, "Like how dogs can hear high-pitched whistles that we can't?"

"Exactly," Mr. Lunis replied. "So, we need to figure out exactly which frequency affects these creatures."

Max frowned, "And once we find it?"

Mr. Lunis sighed, "We'll cross that bridge when we get there. First, let's focus on finding it."

Lila clapped her hands together, "Alright! Let's make some noise!"

Max chuckled, "Literally."

Mr. Lunis pulled out a frequency generator from one of the cupboards. "This device can produce a range of sound frequencies. We'll start low and work our way up. Watch the worm's reaction closely."

Lila leaned in, her nose nearly touching the container, "Ready!"

Max, on the other hand, stood a bit farther away, looking a tad green. "Yeah... ready."

Mr. Lunis turned the dial, and a low hum

filled the room. The worm in the container continued wiggling, unaffected.

Lila squinted, "No change."

Mr. Lunis nodded and increased the frequency. A slightly higher pitch resonated. The worm continued to move as usual.

What felt like several hours and many frequencies later, there was still no noticeable reaction. Lila sighed in frustration, "This is like looking for a needle in a haystack."

Max added, "A very noisy haystack."

Mr. Lunis was about to reply when suddenly, as he turned the dial once more, the worm stiffened. It's wiggling slowed and then stopped altogether. The sound filling the room was a high-pitched, almost musical note.

Lila's eyes widened, "That's it! Look!"

Max inched closer, eyes wide, "It's... frozen."

Mr. Lunis looked satisfied, "This frequency seems to paralyze them, at least temporarily. This is a good start."

Lila grinned, "One step closer to saving the school!"

Max smirked, "And waking up the whole neighborhood with this noise."

Mr. Lunis chuckled, "A small price to pay, I'd say."

As the trio began discussing the next steps, the first rays of morning light shone brightly into the lab, symbolizing the hope that now flickered in their hearts.

CHAPTER 13

THE SOUND OF FREEDOM

The science lab was now filled with the clamor of conversation and machines. Mr. Lunis was engrossed in adjusting the frequency generator. Whilst they had found one frequency that appeared to paralyze the worms, Mr. Lunis was in search of other frequencies that affected the worms in different ways and could also help them. So far, his efforts were drawing a blank. Max, a little fidgety from all the waiting, was tapping his hand rhythmically on his chair.

Lila, drawn to the rhythm from Max's chair, suddenly had an idea. "Hey Max," she called, "Remember that time you said rock music can scare away anything?"

Max raised an eyebrow, "It was a joke, Lila.

Besides, it's not just any rock music. It's MY rock music. The best kind."

Lila giggled, "Oh, let's test that theory, shall we?" Without waiting for a reply, she snatched Max's phone from his pocket and plugged it into the lab's sound system.

Before Max could protest, the loud and roaring beats of his favorite rock song echoed through the room. Mr. Lunis jumped, looking around in surprise.

But the real reaction was from the worm inside the container. It squirmed and wriggled, seemingly in distress, before it scurried to the corner of its container, trying to hide.

Lila laughed out loud, pointing at the worm. "See? Your music does scare creatures away!"

Max crossed his arms, feigning annoyance, but the hint of a smile betrayed him. "Guess I do have good taste after all."

Mr. Lunis, after overcoming the initial surprise, chuckled. "Well, that's unexpected. While it might not be the scientific breakthrough I was hoping for, it's a discovery nonetheless."

Lila, looking triumphant, said, "There you go, Max. Your music could be the secret weapon we've been looking for."

Max grinned, "I always knew my rock collection would save the day someday."

Mr. Lunis smiled, "Lila could be right, Max. This might just be what we need. With this music and the frequency we found earlier, we might just have a shot at defeating these worms!"

Lila turned off the music and handed Max his phone back, "There you go, hero. Keep it safe."

Max winked, "Always do."

With a new energy in the room, the trio got back to work, with rock n' roll as their unexpected ally.

A little later the trio were huddled over a large blueprint of the school. Mr. Lunis, his furry hand tracing the lines, pointed to the central room. "This is the Headmistress' office, where the main controls for the school's PA system are. If we can connect the frequency generator here, we can broadcast the sound throughout the entire school."

Lila's eyes widened. "That will chase away all the worms from the pupils?"

Mr. Lunis nodded. "In theory, yes. If the worms react as we've observed, the sound will make them very uncomfortable, forcing them out."

Max scratched his chin, thinking. "But how do we get everyone together and keep them long enough for the worms to leave? They could suspect something."

Lila grinned, mischief sparkling in her eyes. "Leave that to me. Ever heard of a surprise assembly?"

Max raised an eyebrow. "You're going to trick the entire school into an assembly?"

Lila winked. "Got any better ideas?"

Mr. Lunis chuckled. "It might just work. The element of surprise is crucial. While they're confused, we play our 'music'."

Max smirked. "And by 'music', you mean the ear-piercing frequency and maybe some rock n' roll?"

Lila laughed. "Precisely! Oh, I can't wait to see Mr. Xanar's face."

Mr. Lunis turned serious. "We need to be careful. If Xanar suspects what we're up to, he might try to stop us."

Lila and Max exchanged a determined look. "We won't let him," Max said firmly.

Lila added, "We've got a werewolf science teacher on our side. What could possibly go wrong?"

Mr. Lunis sighed, "I have a feeling I'll regret revealing my secret to you two."

Max grinned, "Probably. But hey, look on the bright side– you've got two awesome sidekicks now."

"Hey!" said Lila, "it's you two who are my sidekicks!" The trio chuckled; the weight of their mission momentarily forgotten.

"Alright," Lila said, clapping her hands together. "Let's do this. Operation Eardrum begins first thing Monday!"

"Does that mean I can sleep in tomorrow?" asked Max hopefully.

"Yes, Max!" answered Lila and Mr. Lunis in unison, before laughing.

"Although," continued Lila, "don't forget our club meeting tomorrow."

"Club meeting?" enquired Mr. Lunis, "what club is that?"

"Zombies Ate My Homework!" answered Lila and Max in unison grinning.

"It's probably best I don't ask!" replied Mr. Lunis, "See you both on Monday!"

CHAPTER 14

NIGHT WHISPERS

Lila's bedroom was the stuff of dreams for most 11-year-olds. Filled with all kinds of toys and contraptions, along with a whole hammock full of stuffed toys (each with its own name and personality), a wall plastered with doodles of ghosts, aliens, and what could only be described as 'mystery creatures', and a shelf overflowing with magazines and newspapers with titles like The Fortean Times, and the Tales of the Paranormal.

Whilst some of these pictures and magazines may have been the stuff of nightmares for some, for Lila it was quite the opposite. It was her cozy retreat- like being wrapped in a warm hug. Yet, despite the comfort and familiarity, sleep was playing hard to get.

She tossed and turned, the glow-in-the-dark stars on her ceiling providing the only light in the room. Every so often, she would hear a distant car, or the howl of a neighborhood dog, and her imagination would instantly turn these mundane sounds into whispers of alien conspiracies or the distant roars of werewolves.

Her mind played scenes from the past few days like a movie on repeat. The worms, the new teacher Mr. Xanar, the unusual behavior of her classmates, and most surprising of all, Mr. Lunis's transformation.

Fluffington Senior, her most cherished teddy bear, seemed to be looking at her with eyes that said, "There, there. Everything will be alright." She clutched him close, burying her face into his soft fur.

She glanced at her digital clock, its numbers glowing a soft blue: 2:37 AM. Groaning, she turned onto her back, staring at the ceiling. "How am I ever going to face tomorrow on no sleep?" she whispered to Fluffington.

Hoping to distract her racing mind, she recalled the tales her grandma used to tell her-of brave heroes and heroines who faced insurmountable odds. Lila remembered the story of Boudicca, the warrior queen who challenged the Roman Empire, becoming a legend of bravery. Then there was Amelia Earhart, who fearlessly flew over oceans and continents, breaking records and challenging the expectations of her time. She remembered how her grandma always emphasized that bravery wasn't the absence of fear, but the ability to move forward despite it.

Replaying her grandma's soothing voice in her head, Lila felt a sense of determination. "Alright, alien worms," she murmured defiantly, "You've met your match."

Lila then came up with a game to help her sleep. 'If I can count backward from a hundred without thinking of worms or aliens, I'll finally drift to sleep.'

'100, 99, 98… alien worm… darn!'

'Okay, again… 100, 99, 98, 97… mysterious Mr. Xanar... Oh no!'

She giggled at her own silly game. On her third attempt, she made it past fifty before her mind conjured another weird image, but by that point, her eyes were heavy.

Lila's thoughts became more disjointed, her worries slowly fading into the background, replaced by dreams of heroics, adventure, and her teddy, Fluffington, piloting a spaceship.

Before she knew it, she was deep in slumber, getting some much needed sleep before facing the challenges of the coming days.

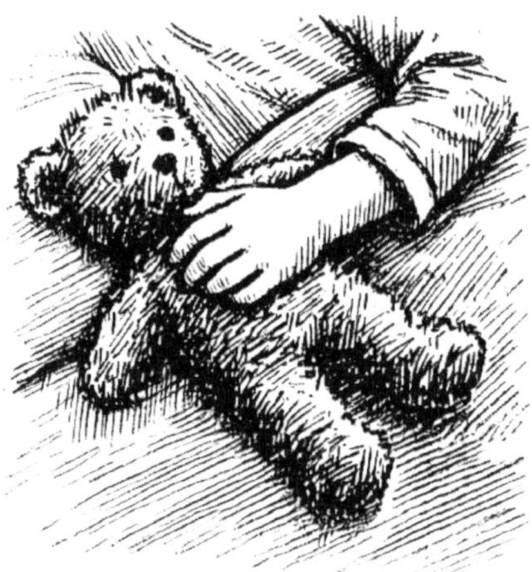

CHAPTER 15

CLUB ORIGINS

It was Sunday morning and sunshine streamed through the gaps in the wooden fence, creating playful patterns on the floor of the secret club den. An old rickety table, a chalkboard with doodles of aliens and monsters, and mismatched chairs made up the décor. A small, barely noticeable, sign hung above the entrance proudly proclaimed, "Zombies Ate My Homework Club – Founding Members: Lila & Max."

Max had arrived early, setting up a little snack corner. He knew that Lila appreciated the little gestures, especially in times of crisis. A bowl of crisps, a couple of cans of coke, and a packet of chocolate covered Oreos awaited her.

Lila burst into the den, excitement radiating off her. "Alright, detective Max, ready for the meeting?" she asked, giving him a playful salute. "Okay so first with the register. Max?"

Max just sat there looking at her with an expression that read, 'do we really need to do this every time?'

"Max," Lila tried again.

"Lila, you know I'm here. I mean it is just us."

"Well, you never know Max. Maybe one day we'll have a few more members. If we survive the next couple of days that is."

As they settled in, opening the packet of biscuits, Lila looked at Max, her eyes filled with nostalgia. "Do you remember the first time you came here, Max?"

Max laughed, "How could I forget? You wheeled me here, insisting I keep my eyes closed, whilst talking about ghosts and goblins as if they were our classmates."

Lila giggled. "Well, I did always have a wild imagination. But you, Mr. New Kid, were the perfect audience."

Max rolled his eyes playfully. "Yeah, because I had no other friends yet and you kidnapped me."

Lila smirked. "You're welcome. Otherwise, you'd have been stuck with all the norms."

Max shuddered dramatically. "Not the 'norms'! Anything but that."

They both burst out laughing.

Max grinned. "I think it all started with that ridiculous excuse of yours for not having your homework."

Lila plopped down on a chair, taking a biscuit. "Of course! The day Mrs. Cobb's face turned the colour of an overripe tomato, and all because I told her that zombies ate my homework."

Max snorted, recalling that fateful day in the classroom. "Oh, it was the talk of the class all week! Everyone was whispering and giggling. I mean, kids come up with the dog excuse or that they simply forgot, but leave it to Lila to come up with zombies munching on her math assignment."

Lila giggled, "I had to keep things interesting, didn't I? But seriously, I had watched this horror film the previous night and just dreamt of zombies all night. So, when I woke up and realized I hadn't done the homework, it just… slipped out!"

Max continued, "Mrs. Cobb's face! I'll never

forget it! She went, 'Lila Thompson! Are you telling me... zombies ate your homework?!' And the whole class burst into laughter. Well, except for Phillip who looked genuinely concerned for his workbook."

"Poor Phillip," mused Lila, thinking about the fact that it was actually alien worms he should have been worried about in regard to his workbook. "But hey, that incident did have a silver lining. It made us friends! You approached me after class and said, 'So, about these homework-eating zombies…' and I knew right then that we'd be partners in crime."

Lila grinned, "And thus, the 'Zombies Ate My Homework' Club was born! Investigating mysteries, sharing spooky tales, and of course, making up fantastic excuses for not doing homework."

"Speaking of which," Max said, mischief sparkling in his eyes, "I doubt we need to come up with an excuse for Monday. Fighting an alien invasion should be good enough, right?"

Lila laughed heartily. "Absolutely! And at least for once, it'll be the truth."

Max softened a bit and said, "But in all seriousness, Lila, I'm glad you 'kidnapped' me that day. I may not completely share your fascination with the paranormal, but we clicked. And look where it's gotten us—fighting real-life alien worms with a werewolf teacher."

They both burst into laughter, feeling the weight of their current situation lift, even if just for a little while. In this den, with their shared memories and unbreakable bond, they felt ready to face any challenge together.

As the laughter subsided, the pair sat back in their chairs, both looking thoughtful. The room's ambiance changed as the golden morning glow was replaced by the grey light of an overcast day. Time passed slowly as they both sat there, lost in their own thoughts.

Max twiddled a pencil between his fingers, "Lila," he began hesitantly, "this alien worm stuff is really scary, right?"

Lila took a deep breath, staring at a doodle of a spaceship she'd drawn months ago. "Yeah, it's really scary," she admitted, her tone soft. "It's one thing to imagine these tales and laugh about them here in our safe little den. But seeing it... it's another thing entirely."

Max looked down at the floor, "You know, when we started this club, I was always secretly relieved our mysteries remained unsolved. The idea of the weird and unexplained staying as just stories was... comforting. It was fun, you know. But now, with these worms and everything else that's happening, everything feels heavier."

The atmosphere grew a bit somber, and they both sat in silence for a few minutes before Max voiced what both of them were feeling. "Are you scared, Lila?"

She nodded, biting her lip. "Yeah, but not just for us. For everyone. I mean, this isn't one of our stories where everything magically resets."

Max sighed. "True… but we've always had each other's backs… managed to face our problems together, haven't we?"

Lila nodded in agreement. "Though there's a difference between our usual school drama, or chasing shadows, than coming face to face with the real thing. But hey," she said, trying to lighten the mood, "we're still here, right? Still breathing, still joking, and still a team."

Max smirked, "We did always say we wanted a real adventure."

Lila smiled back, "And boy, have we got one. But I'm terrified too, Max. What if we can't stop this? What if... what if we also end up being controlled by these worms? I mean this is too much. We're just two kids." Max gulped, the weight of the possibility pressing down on him. But he squared his shoulders and said, "Then we'll fight, Lila. With everything we've got. And with Mr. Lunis on our side, I reckon our odds aren't too shabby."

Lila grinned, "True, having a werewolf teacher does tip the scales a bit in our favor. Still," she hesitated, her eyes shimmering with unshed tears, "promise me something?"

"Anything," Max replied.

"If one of us gets... taken over, the other will save themselves. No point in both of us becoming alien zombies. Deal?"

Max took a deep breath, and after a pause answered "No deal, Lila. I understand what you're saying, but no one gets left behind. Not in the 'Zombies Ate My Homework' club. Wouldn't be much of a club with one member left, would it?"

They held each other's gaze for a moment, before Lila pounced on Max, giving him the biggest hug. Whilst the future of their school, their town, and quite possibly the world, might be hanging in the balance, in that moment, the bond of their friendship felt as powerful as any force in the universe.

CHAPTER 16

DAWN AT DANGER'S DOOR

Monday morning had never felt so ominous. The sun had barely peeked over the horizon, casting the school in a mix of purples and golds. Most of Swindon's children were still tucked away in their beds, dreaming of anything but the perils that lurked in their school's corridors.

Lila's heart raced as she, Max, and the Science Teacher approached the school's entrance. The large double doors, usually a welcoming sight, now appeared menacing.

"Why is that school seems spookier so early in the morning?" Lila whispered, her voice trembling.

"It's not the morning that's the problem," Max replied, shivering despite his thick jacket.

"It's the silence. Usually, there's the sound of kids laughing, teachers chatting, the bell ringing..."

"But now," Mr. Lunis added, also a little unnerved, "it's just our footsteps echoing back at us. And whatever is waiting for us inside."

The group moved stealthily through the corridors. Every shadow made Lila jump, half expecting a transformed pupil or two to pop out, but so far nothing.

"We need to reach the PA system in the Headmistress' office. That's our best shot at broadcasting the frequency," Mr. Lunis reminded them.

Max held up his phone, which had the rock music track ready to play. "And once we play this, we watch the worms run for the hills. You do have a plan for getting everyone in the hall, don't you, Lila?"

"Trust me," said Lila, "I got this."

As they neared the Headmistress' office, they passed by the school's trophy case. In the dim morning light, the golden awards looked like they were casting eerie, elongated shadows.

"Remember when you tried to prove that the school's oldest trophy was haunted?" Max nudged Lila, attempting to lighten the mood.

Lila chuckled, "Oh, don't remind me. Turns out, it was just the caretaker's cat in the case knocking all the trophies."

Mr. Lunis raised an eyebrow, "That sounds like a story for another time."

Suddenly, a shadow moved at the end of the corridor. All three of them froze. But as the shadow got closer, it became clear – it was just the caretaker, Mr. Perkins, as if on demand. As he pushed his cart, he was humming a tune, completely unaware of the impending threat.

Mr. Perkins looked up, suddenly noticing the trio. "Morning," he said gruffly. "A little early for school aren't we?"

"Oh, we're just working on a special project," said Lila quickly. "By the way, these floors are looking lovely, Mr. Perkins."

"Um thank you," answered the caretaker, caught a little off guard. "Special project, eh. Well, just make sure you don't make a mess. Worst thing about this job is all you blooming kids," the last sentence trailing off as he carried on by, his one-eyed cat Juno not far behind.

Mr. Lunis breathed a sigh of relief, "We need to be careful. Not everyone knows about... well, you know."

Lila nodded, "The invasion. Right.

Operation Eardrum is in full swing. Let's get to that office."

They resumed their journey towards the Headmistress' office, the key objective within their grasp, hoping that their plan would be the antidote to the alien menace within.

CHAPTER 17

ART ATTACK

As carefully and quietly as they could manage, they slowly made their way through the school corridors, which were adorned with posters for the upcoming school play– 'Invasion of the Body Snatchers'– which seemed eerily fitting now.

Lila pointed at a poster, whispering, "We don't need a play. We've got the real deal here!"

Suddenly, a door creaked open, revealing a group of pupils with that all-too-familiar blank stare. The trio quickly ducked around a corner.

"Whew! That was close," Lila whispered, wiping the sweat from her brow.

Max peeked around the corner, "Look at them. It's like they're on autopilot."

"You think they're off to another worm-planting party?" Lila mused, trying to lighten the mood.

Mr. Lunis hushed them, "Focus. We need to get to that PA system. I imagine they're not the only ones here, so the sooner we get to that office the better."

They continued sneaking down the corridor, them heading one way, whilst the alien-controlled pupils headed in the other. The three of them were moving slowly and stealthily, half walking backwards as they watched the pupils at the other end of the corridor. Suddenly, Lila kicked a discarded can, the noise echoing throughout the empty hallway. In the distance, the alien-controlled pupils immediately turned their heads in their direction.

"Uh-oh," Lila muttered.

Mr. Lunis quickly motioned for them to follow him into a nearby classroom, locking the door behind them. They all huddled, catching their breath.

Mr. Lunis looked serious, "We need a distraction."

Lila reached into her bag and pulled out a bottle filled with shimmering glitter.

"Really, Lila?" Max exclaimed. "Glitter?

We're being chased by alien zombies, and you think sparkles are the answer?"

Lila smirked, "It's not just any glitter; it's a glitter bomb!" Lila motioned for Mr. Lunis. To unlock the door and then stepped into the hallway. She swiftly twisted the cap, threw the bottle, and a burst of glitter sprayed into the hallway, catching the overhead lights, and creating a dazzling, almost blinding effect.

The alien-controlled pupils stopped, shielding their eyes, and trying to make sense of the sudden disco party in front of them. Lila smirked gesturing towards her bag, "I have everything in here. Always be prepared. That's my motto".

"I have literally never heard you say that before," said Max.

"Well, we have never had an extra-terrestrial invasion on our hands before. It's my new motto!"

Mr. Lunis nodded in approval, "Good job, Lila. Now whilst they're still distracted, let's use the confusion to our advantage."

The hall still a dazzling array of glitter, the trio snuck out of the classroom, making their way further down the hall, inching closer to their target: the Headmistress' office and the

PA system.

CHAPTER 18

THE WORM TURNS

The trio stood outside the door to the Headmistress' office, the revered spot where the school's PA system lay. The door was slightly ajar, and a dim light glowed from within.

Lila inched forward, pressing her ear against the door. "I think it's clear," she whispered.

But as they began to enter, a shadow loomed over them. They turned slowly, meeting the gaze of none other than Mr. Xanar, the school's newest, and now most menacing, teacher. Today, his eyes bore that chilling, alien-infested glow.

"Thought you could outsmart us, did you?" Mr. Xanar's voice was both calm and cold, a combination that sent shivers down Lila's spine.

"Oh, Mr. Xanar! Fancy meeting you here," Lila tried to joke, but her voice trembled a tad. "We were just... um, looking for lost homework?"

Max nudged her. "Really, Lila?"

Mr. Lunis stepped forward, "Mr. Xanar, we need to use the PA system. It's for the ummm class assembly."

The teacher smirked, a disturbing glint in his eyes. "A little noise won't save you now."

With an uneasy but defiant stance, Max questioned, "Why are you doing this, Mr. Xanar? What do you even want?"

A ghastly grin spread across Mr. Xanar's face, eyes flickering with a treacherous gleam. "Isn't it obvious, children?" he sneered, "we've watched, in the depths, waiting for our chance to return. And now this world is ripe for the taking. Your kind is weak and divided. We intend to reign supreme, erasing your puny civilization and crafting a new world under our dominion."

Lila's eyes sparkled with defiance. "Well, Mr. Xanar, you must've missed the lesson on human history. Every time something's tried to knock us down, we've come back stronger. So, bring it on– we're ready!" In the tense pause that followed, Lila sensed a falter in the alien-teacher's certainty, and she pressed on, "besides, Mr. Xanar, did you hear about the alien teacher who tried to take over the world?... He couldn't make the grade!"

Mr. Lunis, seizing the moment, grabbed a nearby chair, positioning it defensively between the three of them and Mr. Xanar.

"Quick, kids! The PA!" he yelled.

As Max and Lila quickly went into the Headmistress' office and tracked down the PA system, the sounds outside of a struggle from Mr. Lunis and Mr. Xanar grew increasingly chaotic. Every second was critical.

Max managed to connect his phone and get the rock music blaring through the school's PA system. The heavy guitar riffs and pounding drums echoed through the corridors, a battle cry against the alien invaders. They could hear the high-pitched squeals of the alien worms, their dominance waning under the powerful sonic assault.

Outside, Mr. Xanar, far from defeated, began to transform into a grotesque, worm-like creature, tentacles writhing, eyes ablaze with malevolent fire. The trio would need more than just courage to survive the imminent, treacherous confrontation that awaited them.

As Max and Lila scrambled with the equipment, they heard the commotion outside. Mr. Lunis was desperately fending off Mr. Xanar. Time was running out.

"Hurry, you two! The frequency!" shouted Mr. Lunis.

Suddenly, the lights in the hallway flickered, creating a haunting pulsating glow. As Max found the right frequency and, Mr. Xanar's horrid transformation took another step.

He expanded in size, and multiple tentacles erupted, replacing his once-human arms. This teacher, previously a figure of authority, morphed into a grotesque, gigantic worm-like monstrosity. Writhing worms within him could be seen through his translucent skin.

"He's too strong! We need something else!" Mr. Lunis howled.

Lila and Max scanned the room, desperately searching for something, anything, that could help. Suddenly, in the corner, Max spotted a guitar on a stand. "Wow! A Gibson Les Paul," remarked Max. "I never would have guessed that Mrs. Lanegan was the type. Cool."

Now is not the time, Max," snapped Lila, "If

you're gonna do what I think you're gonna do, do it already!"

Max grabbed the guitar and plugged it into the PA system. Strumming the guitar with ferocity generated waves of sound that made the creature recoil with each note. Inspired, Max belted out, "Mr. Xanar, you may teach math, but you can't count on winning this!"

Lila joined the musical fray, singing, "You've got the tentacles, but we've got the decibels!"

The tentacled, wormy monstrosity, though fierce, hesitated, seemingly disoriented. With Max's guitar skills, Lila's sassy singing, and Mr. Lunis's werewolf prowess, the creature was on the back foot.

With a final, electrifying guitar solo from Max, the creature, unable to bear the musical onslaught, exploded into a shower of green sludge.

After a brief moment of shock, Lila and Max rushed to Mr. Lunis's side, helping him up. The air was thick with relief.

"You kids did great," Mr. Lunis said with a weary smile.

Covered in alien goo, the trio stared at where Mr. Xanar once stood.

Lila, wiping slime off her face, joked, "Guess

he wasn't ready for our talent show act, huh?"

Max, also trying to clean the green slime from his face, laughed, "I tell you what though. I am never eating jelly from the school canteen again. This is disgusting!"

"So is the food from the canteen!" chipped in Lila.

CHAPTER 19

WORMAGEDDON

The shrill music echoed throughout the empty halls; every corner alive with the sound of the guitar riffs that had been their savior. As Lila, Max, and Mr. Lunis quickly made their way back through the school, they were met with a sight that would've made anyone's stomach churn. The floor was writhing, covered with the squirming alien worms that seemed to be in pain from the music.

"Oh gross," Max muttered, stepping carefully to avoid squashing any. "It's like a horror movie out here. Wormageddon!"

Lila looked at the masses of worms, her nose wrinkling. "We can't leave them here. What do we do now?"

Mr. Lunis knelt down, cautiously examining

one of the worms that had separated from the pulsating mass. "It seems the frequencies did more than we anticipated. They're in a state of distress."

Lila frowned, her compassionate nature bubbling up. "I know they're alien invader thingies... but it feels kind of wrong to see them like this."

A soft gust of wind signaled the entrance doors of the school bursting open.

In marched two men, their black suits so crisp they might've been ironed mere minutes ago. Their shiny shoes clicked rhythmically on the floor, and their reflective sunglasses hid any trace of emotion. Behind them, a team wearing hazmat suits, gloves, and masks held peculiar containers that looked like they had jumped straight out of a sci-fi movie.

Like a well-oiled machine, the hazmat team that followed started scooping the writhing worms into the containers, their actions swift and precise.

Lila, Max, and Mr. Lunis exchanged confused glances. "Who called the cleanup crew?" Max whispered.

Max's voice dropped to a whisper; his eyes fixed on the newcomers. "I've seen enough movies to know that men in black are never a good sign."

Without missing a beat, the hazmat-suited individuals continued their methodical dance of collecting worms. They seemed trained for this exact task, scooping up the creatures with surprising gentleness and depositing them into strange containers, which emitted a soft blue glow upon closure.

The efficiency of the cleanup was unnerving. Lila exchanged glances with her two companions, the weight of unasked questions evident in her eyes. Who were these people? How did they know about the worms? Were they friends or foes?

Max nudged Lila and pointed discreetly at the badges on the hazmat suits - a peculiar symbol resembling a worm inside a shield. It was clear that this wasn't their first worm rodeo.

Lila took a deep breath, her determination rekindling. "We need answers. And I have a feeling those men in black might have them."

CHAPTER 20

MEN IN BLACK

The fluorescent lights of the school cast an eerie glow on the pristine suits of the two men, who stood slightly apart, surveying the scene. The silence between them was palpable. The only lucid souls in that vast sea of confusion seemed to be Lila, Max, and Mr. Lunis, with the rest of the school's population dazedly wandering like sleepwalkers awakened mid-dream.

The first man in black, a taller figure with a chiseled jawline visible even beneath his sunglasses, pointed towards the trio. "You three, come here."

Lila, confidence bubbling, stepped forward. "Who are you guys?"

The second man, slightly shorter with an air

of authority, cleared his throat. "First, tell us who's in charge here."

Lila, with a mix of bravado and jest, placed a hand on her chest. "Me, I guess." She gave a smirk, "Unless you want to chat with the leader of these alien worms. He's kind of all over the place, though."

Max snorted, clearly appreciating Lila's attempt at humor amidst the chaos. Even Mr. Lunis allowed himself a tiny smile, his canine teeth peeking out just slightly.

The taller man's expression didn't waver, but there was a hint of amusement in his voice. "Quite the brave one, aren't you? You can call me Agent Steele, and this is Agent Frost."

Agent Frost, with a nod towards the hazmat team, said, "This is a containment crew from the Department of Health. We're here for... pest control."

Lila raised an eyebrow. "Pest control? Those are alien worms, not rats."

Agent Steele sighed. "That's a more... digestible explanation for the general public."

Max leaned in, whispering to Lila but loud enough for the agents to hear, "I think their dictionary's missing the word 'subtle'."

Agent Frost's lips twitched, the closest thing

to a smile. "We appreciate your efforts. The situation here seems... contained."

Mr. Lunis frowned. "How did you know to come here? And how did you get here so quickly?"

Agent Steele pointed to a tiny device in his ear. "We have our methods. We've been monitoring such... disturbances."

Lila's eyes darted between the two agents. "So, what happens next?"

Agent Steele straightened, his voice taking on a more official tone. "The school will be closed for a week. Officially, for pest control." He glanced at the dazed teachers and pupils. "They won't remember much, just that they had a very... strange dream."

Lila glanced back at her school, turned upside-down. It was difficult to digest how quickly things had changed. With a sigh, she met Agent Steele's gaze. "And us?"

Agent Steele smirked, "Oh, you'll remember. You three are too entwined in this. Just... try not to spread panic. And enjoy the extra holiday."

Max grinned. "Our lips are sealed. As long as the aliens stay out of them."

As the trio turned to leave, the team around

them focusing on the cleanup, Lila felt a tap on her shoulder. She turned to see Agent Steele extending a card - a simple white card with an embossed number.

"Call this if you come across any more... pests," he whispered.

Lila nodded, a mix of trepidation and excitement building in her chest. "We will."

The agents and their crew, having cleared all the nearby writhing worms, moved on elsewhere, leaving the entrance hall eerily silent. The trio, still processing everything, began to walk towards the exit.

Mr. Lunis cleared his throat, "Okay, milkshake, anyone? My treat, of course."

"Maybe we should go get cleaned up first," suggested Max, still wiping remnants of the goo from his chair.

Lila and Max exchanged a smile. It was an odd ending to an even odder day. But in the midst of the alien chaos, some things, like the bond of friendship, remained wonderfully constant.

Just as they were about to leave, Mr. Perkins, the caretaker, stepped through the doors, his mop and bucket beside him. "Oh, for goodness' sake. Look at all this mess! There goes my lunchbreak!" Strangely, he didn't seem at all surprised by the men in suits, the cleanup team, or all the bewildered pupils wandering around.

CHAPTER 21

BACK TO THE GRIND

The school bell rang its familiar chime, echoing through the hallways of Swindon Academy. Pupils flooded out of classrooms, a sea of chatter, and laughter. The typical buzz of school life was back.

Lila walked through the corridor, her school bag slung over her shoulder, a bemused smile playing on her lips. All around her, pupils were discussing typical school topics: homework, football games, the latest episode of Celebrities We Barely Remember Singing and Dancing Whilst Wearing Masks.

Not a single person mentioned alien worms. Nor was there anything mentioned on the news. Not even one comment on the school being closed the week before. It was as if the entire episode had been erased from existence.

Lila reached her locker, and as she twiddled the combination into place, she caught a familiar voice. "Psst! Lila!"

Turning, she saw Max grinning at her from behind a tall potted plant. He wheeled himself out, revealing a mischievous look in his eyes. "Doesn't this feel... weird?"

Lila laughed. "Totally. It's like we're in a parallel universe where last week never happened."

Max nodded, "Even Mrs. Cobb didn't mention anything about 'missing homework' or 'unusual absences'." He paused, "Actually, now that I think about it, that's super weird for her."

Lila chuckled, "Maybe she's been replaced by an alien clone."

"We can only hope," said Max. "Actually no, I think we've had our fair share of aliens. In comparison, Mrs. Cobb is a treat." The two chuckled, then their banter was interrupted by someone clearing their throat. From behind them, Mr. Lunis appeared, his tie slightly askew. "You two certainly seem chipper. Remembering a joke, perhaps?"

Max, with a wink, replied, "Something about

zombies eating homework?"

Mr. Lunis's eyes twinkled, "Ah, that one never gets old. But jokes aside, it's remarkable how quickly things have returned to normal. Almost... too quickly."

Lila furrowed her brow, "You think there's something fishy going on?"

The werewolf teacher shrugged, "I don't know. I just find it odd. But then again, I find many things about human behavior odd." He gave a lopsided grin, revealing a hint of his sharp canines.

Max chuckled, "Like wearing socks with sandals?"

Mr. Lunis laughed, "Precisely! But in all seriousness, just keep your eyes and ears open, alright? Sometimes things aren't as they seem, as you guys already know."

Lila nodded, "We will. Thanks, Mr. L."

With a final wave, the trio parted ways, each heading off to their respective classes. As Lila and Max headed to class, Lila felt a nagging sensation, a feeling that the calm was perhaps just the eye of a larger storm. But for now, she pushed it to the back of her mind. After all, there were tests to study for, and friends to catch up with, and probably some forgotten homework that she needed to do.

The mundane routine of school life awaited, but as Lila was soon coming to understand, there was never a dull moment at Swindon Academy.

CHAPTER 22

MYTHS AND MONSTERS

The day wore on, and soon it was the last period of the day: English Literature with Mr. Kumar. Or at least, that's what the schedule said. But when Lila and Max entered the classroom, they were met with a surprise.

The familiar figure of Mr. Kumar was absent. Instead, standing at the front of the class, adjusting some books, was none other than Mr. Lunis.

The classroom buzzed with confusion.

"Why's the Science Teacher teaching English?" whispered Jenny from the back row.

"Maybe Mr. Kumar is sick?" suggested Russell, pushing up his glasses.

But Lila and Max exchanged a knowing glance. They had a hunch this was no ordinary substitute situation.

As the bell rang, Mr. Lunis cleared his throat, silencing the class. "Good afternoon, everyone. Mr. Kumar had an... unexpected engagement and asked if I could fill in for today. I have no idea where you folks left off. So today, we're going to start with something completely different, and look at myths and legends, and the differences between legend and history."

The class moaned collectively. Well, aside from Lila and Max. But Mr. Lunis simply smirked and began his lesson, throwing in odd and entertaining anecdotes about werewolves and vampires that kept everyone laughing and engaged.

After the lesson, while most pupils raced towards the exit, eager to begin their evening, Lila and Max approached the teacher's desk.

"Monsters, Mr. Lunis?" Lila said, an eyebrow raised in amusement. "Really?"

Mr. Lunis grinned sheepishly. "I had to improvise. And besides, who better to teach about these things than a real-life werewolf?"

Max chuckled, "Point taken. But... why are you really here? And where's Mr. Kumar."

Mr. Lunis glanced around, ensuring no one was within earshot. "I honestly am not sure what happened with Mr. Kumar. But as soon as I heard that they wouldn't be here for the foreseeable, I offered to step in. I've decided to keep a closer eye on things. Just in case."

Lila frowned, "You think there's more to come?"

The werewolf teacher sighed. "I don't know, Lila. But after what happened... I felt it was my duty to be here, for both of you. To be your secret guardian."

Lila's eyes softened. "Thank you, Mr. Lunis. It means a lot."

He smiled, patting both kids on the back. "Just remember, always be vigilant. And if anything... 'out of the ordinary' happens, you know where to find me."

Max grinned, "Teaching about monsters in an English class?"

Mr. Lunis chuckled, "Exactly."

As the duo left the classroom, the weight on their shoulders felt a little lighter, knowing they had an ally looking out for them. But the mystery of the school's sudden return to normalcy remained, alongside that of the missing English teacher.

CHAPTER 23

THE ULTIMATE EXCUSE

The afternoon sun streamed through the windows of the Zombies Ate My Homework Club den. Lila and Max sat on the mismatched beanbags they'd claimed as their personal thrones, flipping through old notebooks.

"These were some good times," Max mused, pointing to an entry titled 'The Haunted Library Book'. "Remember that one? The book that always turned its pages when no one was looking?"

Lila laughed, "Oh yes! We staked out the library for three nights before realizing it was just the caretakers' cat…again!"

"And then there's this one," Max continued, pointing to another titled 'The Phantom Ringing'. "The phone that kept ringing in the middle of the night, even though it was unplugged."

Lila snorted, "Turned out to be a faulty alarm clock in the next room. We have had our fair share of duds."

"But think about it, Lila," Max said, leaning in with a mischievous glint in his eyes. "We now have the ultimate reason for not doing our homework."

Lila grinned, catching on immediately. "Oh? And what would that be?"

Max dramatically opened a new page in their record book, writing in bold, capital letters: "ALIEN INVASION."

Lila laughed heartily. "Oh, that's perfect! Just imagine the look on Mrs. Cobb's face when we tell her we couldn't do our math homework because of an alien invasion!"

"And the best part?" Max added, winking. "This time, it's actually true!"

The two friends burst into fits of laughter, imagining the baffled expression of their teacher.

"Though," Lila mused, once the laughter had subsided, "it's going to be hard to top this one."

Max nodded in agreement, "Yeah, 'Alien

Worms' is definitely going down in club history."

Their light-hearted banter continued for a while, until Max suddenly became quiet, clearly something on his mind.

"Lila, there's one thing about this alien invasion that I don't quite understand."

"Just the one thing?" asked Lila raising her eyebrows questioningly.

"Well, a few, of course. But one thing in particular. We keep calling them alien worms. But remember when we were confronted by Mr. Xanar, before we managed to set up the PA system?"

"You mean right before he grew all those tentacles, and then exploded?"

"Yeah. He talked about coming from the depths…returning. It was as if they weren't from another planet at all…but this one."

Lila chewed on her lip, deep in thought. "You know, now that you mention it, it did sound weird…like they were here all along. But if that's true, where have they been hiding all this time?"

Max shrugged, "The depths could mean anywhere - deep in the oceans, underground, or maybe even a hidden dimension. Who knows?"

Lila frowned. "And why now? Why did they decide to make their move now? It's all just so confusing."

Max sighed, "There's a lot we still don't understand, Lila. But one thing's for sure, we need to be prepared for anything. Because if there's one thing this experience has taught us, it's that Swindon is full of mysteries."

Lila nodded; her expression resolute. "Whatever comes next, we'll face it together. Alien worms, werewolf teachers, or whatever other weirdness this town throws at us."

The two friends exchanged a determined look. But neither could shake off the unsettling feeling that this was just the beginning of their adventures.

And with that, a chapter in their lives closed, but the storybook of Swindon's hidden mysteries had only just opened.

CHAPTER 24

THE MYSTERIOUS NOTE

The bell above the school entrance jingled merrily as pupils flooded out, marking the end of yet another, thankfully, quiet and mundane week. The alien invasion, seemingly forgotten by everyone else, seemed to be fading away, like a dream fading in the morning light.

Lila, her backpack slung over one shoulder, having already bid farewell to Max, walked toward the school gate. However, she suddenly stopped and turned around. Instead of going home like everyone else, she made her way toward the clubhouse. That nagging sensation had returned, and she wasn't ready to head home just yet.

In the clubhouse, Lila threw herself down on a beanbag, and gazed out of the window, the memory of the eerie worms and the bewildering events at school replaying in her mind. It felt like a distant, bizarre dream, yet the faint hum of the rock music and the squirming image of worms remained vivid in her memory. She shivered involuntarily.

But life had resumed its usual pace. The school bell rang on time, homework piled up, and the occasional giggle and chatter filled the hallways of the school. But beneath the veneer of normalcy, Lila felt a peculiar unease. There were moments, fleeting yet palpable, where she felt the lingering presence of something unseen, unheard, and unspoken.

Her eyes wandered across the room, pausing at the framed picture of her and Max. She smiled, her heart swelling with appreciation for the friendship that had tethered her through the surreal ordeal.

As Lila turned back towards the window, she noticed a small, crumpled piece of paper wedged between the windowpane and the sill. Curiosity piquing her, she got up from the beanbag, went outside, and pried the paper from its hidden spot and carefully unfolded it.

Her eyes widened as she read the hastily scrawled message inside:

THEY ARE NOT GONE.
THE WORMS WERE
JUST THE BEGINNING.

BEWARE.

A chill ran down Lila's spine as she reread the words, each syllable sinking with a daunting echo into her consciousness.

Lila's mind raced, questions spilling over each other. Who sent this note? What did it mean? Were the creatures truly not gone? And what did it mean that this was just the beginning? The note was cryptic, shrouded in mystery, and it seemed to beckon them towards another unseen, possibly dangerous, journey.

Lila knew one thing for sure: this note, inscribed with its foreboding message, was a new case for the Zombies Ate My Homework Club. And yet, the shadows of the recent past lingered heavily in her mind, casting a dark veil over this new mystery.

She sighed, glancing once more at the serene sky outside, now darkening with the advancing night. An eerie stillness lingered in the air, as if the universe itself was holding its breath, waiting, watching.

Lila clutched the note, determination flickering in her eyes. Whatever this new mystery was, whatever dangers it hinted at, she and Max – and their secret guardian – would face it together, just like they had faced the unnerving menace before.

But the note also sparked a sliver of excitement within her. After all, mysteries were the lifeblood of their club, and Lila could never resist the lure of the unknown, the unseen, and the unexplained.

She pulled out her phone, typing a quick message to Max, her fingers trembling slightly over the screen.

*"Emergency meeting. Zombies Ate My Homework Club. Tomorrow. We have a new case."

And so, beneath the quiet, unsuspecting veil of the night, a new chapter awaited, teeming with unseen mysteries, unforeseen dangers, and adventures yet to be uncovered.

Stay tuned for their next chapter of mysteries and adventures in the unseen, unheard, and unspoken realms of the unknown.

ABOUT THE AUTHOR

Paul Wennersberg-Løvholen weaves captivating tales for children that have garnered widespread acclaim. One of his standout works is the beloved children's book, "Super Farty Pants," which has captured the hearts of young readers everywhere. In addition to this cherished gem, he has authored several other delightful children's books. Before venturing into the realm of children's literature, Paul's creative pursuits led him down diverse paths, from film, to horror writing. However, life took a turn when he welcomed his own little monsters into the world, inspiring him to embark on a new journey as a children's author. Originally hailing from Wales, Paul now calls Norway his home, balancing his time between family, writing, and working in schools.

Printed in Great Britain
by Amazon

47397383R00067